D0629051

ALSO BY PAUL CORNELL

ROSEBUD
PAUL CORNELL

A TOM DOHERTY ASSOCIATES BOOK

NEW YORK

ROSEBUD

Cover art by Jim Tierney
Cover design by Christine Foltzer

Edited by Ellen Datlow

A Tordotcom Book
Published by Tom Doherty Associates
120 Broadway
New York, NY 10271

www.tor.com

Tor® is a registered trademark of Macmillan Publishing Group, LLC.

ISBN 978-1-250-76540-6 (ebook)
ISBN 978-1-250-76539-0 (trade paperback)

First Edition: 2022

I'd like to thank Stewart Hotston for his physics advice, and also Cheryl Morgan and Ashley Lauren Rogers. Please note, this book includes a depiction of in-universe institutionalized transphobia that may be triggering for some readers.

Rosebud

1

The *Rosebud* makes steady progress along the Saturn side of the Maxwell Gap, in the C Ring, slightly above the mean plane of the system. Here most of the particles are less than 1mm across. So the *Rosebud* is right at home, a shiny red droplet of about the same size. She glides, surveying particles, rocks, and aspiring moonlets, leaving delicate gravitational suggestions in her wake, bundling minerals in the certainty, chaos willing, boulders of titanium and water ice and the like will accumulate and make their way, on precise trajectories, steadily sunward.

This isn't an automated process. The *Rosebud* is a crewed ship, and that crew make *decisions*. That crew can be *blamed* if one of those rocks doesn't end up getting caught by one of the Company tugs in Mars's orbit, but instead ends up, say, destroying Rio de Janeiro.

So the crew of the *Rosebud* are really pretty damn *careful*.

They weren't born careful. Not that all of them *were* born. They've been made careful by experience. By terrible, terrible experience.

The crew of the *Rosebud* are, currently—and by force of law—a balloon, a goth, some sort of science aristocrat possibly, a ball of hands, and a swarm of insects. Well, all of the above but in a handy digital format. They've been called by the ship itself to gather in their shared space to discuss something unusual which has just been picked up by the ship's mineral identification spectrometers. The shared space is, currently, wallpapered as a "1990s boho crashpad." It's supposedly a standard design option, drawn from some Western European human being's genetic memory. But it has a personal flavour about it, a forbidden flavour. And so maybe that's why none of the crew have objected to it and none of them have even mentioned it, because the conversation might lead to awkward places, and anyway it's been the design for a couple of decades now.

Right now, past the beanbags and the context-free lava lamp and the poster of someone called Winona Ryder, a fiery black stallion that is literally on fire is galloping into the room. "Hold, damn you!" shouts Haunt, leaping off the horse as he says it, chiefly because he's just realised "woah" isn't the sort of thing he wants to be heard saying. The horse, being part of Haunt, goes with it, rearing up dramatically, galloping around him once, as the beanbags slide swiftly back to accommodate the animal, and then roaring off in the direction it came only to vanish in a puff of sulphurous smoke. The smoke then sneaks back to quietly rejoin his virtual form.

Haunt dusts his black gloves together and makes a hearty "huh" sound in the back of his throat. He pulls his swagger stick with the skull top from the air and secures it under one armpit. He's pleased that, through the artifices of the ship's central drama register, he's first here. That takes doing. The ship, which is a lesser consciousness, dealing in instincts and gut feelings entirely generated by its conditioning, usually goes with whoever's version of reality seems most social and everyday. It has an absurdly inflated sense of danger. Even the crashpad seems to worry it. It's always tidying. Haunt's love of rebellion, therefore, leads him into creating little dramas, as with the horse. He also likes to win. Hence his pleasure at getting here before the others.

Except then Diana rises from one of the benches, where she must have been lying, and waves her hand in a little circular motion, like she's the queen of something. "Diddly dah," she says. "*I've* been waiting *ages*."

"How?" demands Haunt, hoping his eyebrows are clear enough above his shades that she can see he's raising one.

"Elegantly," she purrs.

"Go on, thump her," says Bob, drifting in on a self-activated breeze that's not particularly urgent. Today

11

Bob is a fetching shade of purple, and he's wearing a black ribbon around his nozzle. Not that he likes it being called that. "Teach her a fucking lesson."

Haunt raises his hands and takes a step back. He has, on various occasions over the years, felt he might teach several fellow crew members a fucking lesson, but that's never been prompted by the suggestions of Bob. He's been dragged away from *Rendezvous with Rama* to be here, and if this is where he has to be, he wants to make every moment of his precious time its own act of artistic rebellion. Diana puts her hand on her chin and sighs at Bob like that's the most utterly dismissible thing anyone's ever said about her. Neither of them feel anything as polite as a reply is in order.

So, with the possibility of Planck-speed violence from Bob—whatever that could possibly involve—still in the air, like he is, it's just as well that at that moment in rolls Huge If True, their uppermost hands all waving desperately as they rush down the polished wooden tiles, their familiar pitter-patter turned into a sound like a rainstorm by their urgency. "Mistakes were made," they say. "I am all out of fucks to give. I'm not willing to discuss it."

"Are you going on about why the ship's called us here?" asks Bob. "If you are, tell, 'cos I've had enough of you lot already."

"No. Or, because I don't know what this is about,

maybe I should say maybe? It all seems very urgent, though."

"All hands on deck," says Diana, with an eyebrow raise toward Huge.

Huge's topmost appendages give her several fingers.

That's when Alonquin Systems Pristine Sound Megasphere Duke Pantomime Hardy the Third enters. Which is ridiculously late, really, because they're the casting vote on all things. For some reason. Well, because the Company like them more than anyone else. It's only their first few representatives which buzz in, like bullets, hitting the far wall and sliding down, dazed, just to establish a presence and the ability to listen in before the whole swarm surges grandly in. Haunt likes to think of them as Quin, because those titles are entirely bought, very cheaply, and would, on Earth, gain Quin zero privilege and entry to precisely nothing. Of course. Because if any of them were the sort of person who could gain entry to anything on Earth, that's where they'd be. And yet, the titles. Gah.

"Order and structure!" yells Quin, their hive cultural greeting booming from their fictional mouth. "We gather again so soon. We were in private time. Very private. You surprise us. What brings us?"

"Mate," says Bob, "none of these fuckers were going to do it, so I thought fuck it." And he makes a little motion to and fro, which is his gesture of bringing, and brings into the space the pre-thought data from the ship's feelings concerning a nearby . . . whatever it is. They all stare at the charts and the graphs until the data resolves into an actual visual image, which it does with the faint air of patronisation the ship always brings to that process, despite it having the intelligence of a happy dog. That's the sort of thing this crew can expect to be patronised by.

"Well," says Diana, "that is not the usual sort of rock."

Because in the space in front of them is the just about real image of what the *Rosebud* is steadily approaching, something else that's sitting above Saturn's C ring. It looks like a planet or moon, but a perfect one, a completely black sphere with no surface detail. "Is there something wrong with the image?" asks Haunt. "That thing doesn't seem to be reflecting any light." They all have an offhand knowledge of where sunward is. It's where all their business is directed to and from, Earth and its subordinate rocky worlds, where their masters are. Out here the sun is small, but still significant. This thing is completely black, an emptiness, like a child's idea of a black hole. There is none more black.

"Am I tripping?" asks Huge. "Not that I do that. I mean, how could I? And of course I wouldn't even if I could. But look at that thing."

"Nothing on the register," says Quin, who's mentally consulted it now, as the shared blip of no secrets when it comes to flying the ship informs them all. "It could be a wreck which has wandered here."

"The wreck of what?" says Diana. "How big is it?" Which turns out to be a rhetorical question because she's already pulling in the answer. The craft is small enough to be brought inside the *Rosebud*, it turns out, a pebble amongst pebbles. "Well, this is interesting," she says. "Spherical, at that size, is very strange. This object isn't massive enough to attain that shape through gravitational attrition. And the friction of space is the friction of impacts. It's not like it's been polished by an ocean."

"No navigation lights, not broadcasting any markers," says Quin.

"You amaze me," growls Haunt.

"Oh God. Maybe it's just really old? Like it's been smoothed and smoothed by the microscopic impact processes here, in a way which nothing else has been, ever? And this explains the weird light thing because it's made of some exotic material, and so maybe it could be valuable?" suggests Huge, their upper fingers fluttering nervously. The gesture is speaking for what they're all feeling. Because this is a scenario Haunt knows from many, many triumph epics. This is the Solar Company discovering a mysterious object in space and boldly boarding it only to find—

"Obviously, it's aliens," says Diana. But who can unpack how much she means it, considering the multiple layers of wryness in which she cloaks every sentence?

Still, it's what they're all thinking. Despite the fact that they'd be the worst possible people to discover such an artefact, because they're not the captain and crew of an SC Man of War. They're just a bunch of program grit.

"Wait a sec, wait a sec, look at the state of this," says Bob, moving up and down to view various aspects of the data at a speed no balloon in real space could manage. His shape is made to contort by the shared values of the space, so he appears to be wiggling up and down through the air like a caterpillar with VTOL capability. "What's the fucker doing?"

Haunt sees the object is reacting a little. Even at maximum magnification it's hard to see exactly what's going on. The spectrum around it is shifting slightly.

"If it's deploying weapons," says Huge, "we're screwed. Time to kiss your ass goodbye, Bob. I am so glad I lived to see you pop. So long, everyone else."

"Right, we're gonna fire back then?" says Bob. "First, like?"

"Wait," snarls Haunt. He realises, to his great pleasure and amazement, that they all actually are. Even Quin. He must have got the tone of command exactly right. He's been absorbing the right ancient dramas. He's older than any of them, and his references, being a product of culture rather than of organic life or artificial intelligence, are entirely different and were really ferociously dated even when he was created, and thus none of them have ever previously seen fit to listen to anything he has to say. "It is easy to jump to conclusions. For some of us, it's the only form of exercise. They may not be bringing up weapons. We are not certain they have even seen us. We are, after all, as tiny as they are."

"Besides," sighs Diana, "the only aggressive response we have is to very slowly make a big dumb object and throw it at them."

"Fuck, really?" says Bob.

"Some of us," sighs Diana, "like to read the manual."

"It could be," says Quin, "some clever competitor, some rebel intent on depriving the Solar Company of its rightful spoils."

That doesn't sound exactly like Quin's usual voice because it's one of the many standard responses the Company have stirred into them over the years. Quin may have put a bit of relish into it, though. Haunt finds himself nodding, and that's fine, because this is a sentiment he, of course, entirely shares.

"A very small-time operator," says Diana.

"It could be a drone," says Haunt. "Left behind for a crewed ship, doing exactly what we're doing. I don't fully believe it even as I say it, but the possibility does exist."

"Surreal physics pirates or aliens then," says Huge. "Which way do we want to get fucked?"

Everyone is silent. Both options are equally worrying. Both options will bring the attention of the Company, which would of course be brilliant, because the Company do their best to bring peace and prosperity to human beings throughout the solar system and it'd be great to see them again, and . . . Haunt feels the familiar prestamped phrases automatically fast-forwarding through his mind, and though he's set his mind to always run them on fast-forward, because the words themselves bore him now, the litany itself is like a lovely old familiar song which takes him back to some round, warm, dark place of the lost past. It's like his shows and his books and his memorabilia. It puts a grim smile on his chiselled features. He looks around and sees the others that have faces are also smiling. And Huge has something like a mouth arc rippling along their midhands. But still, he can feel a lot of fast-forwarding going on.

They all stop at the same instant and make embarrassed noises and return to frowning at the problem ahead of them. Haunt now feels happier about what would happen if they caught the attention of the Company, but still doesn't want to actually do it, not if he doesn't have to. What's that about? It's a question he's often come back to. You'd think he'd want to catch their attention and attract their praise, right? And he does, he does. It would just bring with it such . . . faff. Reactions like that, including the fast-forwarding, are probably a shared joke in Company lore. After a few centuries, it's just what crews like this tend to do. Haunt has a picture in his head of Company officers pretending to be stern about it, with little secret smiles on their faces, and that image makes him feel better too. He attaches the picture, which is a standard image file his unconscious brings out at times of stress, to his inner board, so it'll stay put in his imagination for a while.

"We have prevented the *Rosebud* from going with its gut," says Quin. "Let us keep the glory for this crew and present the Company with a triumph. No signal will be sent sunward until we have explored and identified the object."

"Explored?" says Huge, stretching the word to the limit of plausibility. "Shit. No, really? That's your reaction? If that is a pirate ship, they'll want to erase us!"

"Yeah, and so might aliens," says Bob. "Can we get this done? I'm busy. Stuff. Goings-on."

"I'm sure your games are very important," says Diana.

"One of these days I'm going to fuck you up properly," says Bob.

"What are you going to do, rub against me and frizz my hair?"

Bob makes a noise which Haunt has come to recognise as a psychotic cry of impotent sorrow and rage, but which sounds, in so much as the collective space translates any nonverbal information into its best guess at appropriate audio, like the air being released from a balloon. "I do so appreciate," he says, "how you never let him down gently."

"Yes, yes, let's all avoid the issue of the aliens or pirates deleting us!" says Huge.

Haunt speaks up again and is again inwardly astonished he's gaining such traction. "I hate to say it, but Quin is correct. If the Company begin to pay attention to the situation, it is vital we have been seen to engage usefully with the object. Only that will win us plaudits. Only that allows us even the faint possibility . . ." He doesn't want to finish the sentence, but he's come this far and none of the others is going to dare to voice the same hope. None of them is as rebellious by nature as he is. "Of being noticed in a positive way and having our situation assessed. To be the first crew to retrieve alien tech for the Company is surely our last chance of reward. We have, after all, been out here for over three hundred years."

"Oh," says Huge. "Oh, so we have to risk our existences and hope we're seen as heroes? I see it, I see it, it's obviously the right thing, but . . ." It's odd Huge seems to be struggling so much. If Haunt didn't know better, he'd take them for a free agent.

"Everyone," says Quin, "shall we move the ship closer and begin an exploration that is very careful?" There's a chorus of mixed yes and not yet, with some of the crew going so far as to register a formal vote. The negative ballots are allowed, so the Company must be willing to show a bit of leeway in situations like this. It knows the length of leash that allows crews maximum productivity. That's why it's lasted so long and why they're all basically happy here, even after such a long mission. "It is agreed then," says Quin before all the words have even been uttered and before the last vote has popped into cartoon life, waving desperately. Haunt has often asked who made Quin captain. They're all offhandedly sure someone has, but the paperwork has never been found. They're meant to interact, decide, vote—on everything. That's why there are five of them. That's why they have separate personalities, why they're actual people rather than devolved aspects of the ship. Haunt has heard that's sometimes the case on other grit craft. The thought makes him shiver in his big black many-buckled boots. They could all still end up as that, if they put a foot wrong. If the Company misinterpret their loyal boldness as wilfulness. That's why, in all their time out here, they haven't put a foot at all. After all, several of them put several feet wrong, back in the day. And they're all still living down the shame.

Nobody, in the end, argues. The *Rosebud* exudes a few

more ions, drawn from the great reservoir in the extra dimensions it's connected to, a resource the crew have come to call "the next world." The ship gently accelerates toward the object.

The sphere, *Rosebud* suggests as they draw closer, could indeed be brought into the ship. A docking port and hangar can be created in order to take it in and examine it. And indeed, that's what would probably happen if it was being encountered by actual humans. By many, many actual humans, and their Man of War, none of whom would be scared shitless. There's the show version again. That's how this is supposed to go. Doing it on their own is above their pay grades. Not that they're paid. This is big people stuff. Haunt catches them all checking each other's demeanour. The situation is somehow wrong, because of them not meeting media expectations, while being right, in that they're nevertheless meeting Company expectations. Probably. They are venturing into an enormous void of probably. It itches. It rankles. The impossibility of what's ahead of them adds to the questions which, perhaps, should now be urgently passed to someone more senior. The unending blankness of the sphere should be, if this is indeed an old object, red with the decay of the solar system, pockmarked with micro craters, covered in the dust of moonlets, encrusted with water ice. Instead, it's smoothly above all that. And in approaching it, they're trying to be above their own situation too. Probably.

Haunt is swinging toward the nonhuman possibility for the object's owners because there's no sign of any external identification, and humans love signing the things they own, as they all know from their own interior structures. "Are they deploying sensors of some kind?" he asks. "If these are aliens, I wonder what they make of us, compared to whatever they are?"

"Not pirates, then?" says Bob.

"Definitely aliens," whispers Diana, trying to wind him up. "Because I can't sense any sensors."

"I hope they look like us," says Huge.

The others all turn to look at them. "If they do," says Diana, "I'd be *horrified*."

———

The *Rosebud* purrs up to the sphere. Not that one could hear it purring in space, that's just the sound the ship makes to itself, and the crew have either got used to it or it annoys every fibre of their quasi-beings, continuously.

There's suddenly an alarm, which they all feel in

their very structures. They look around wildly at each other. Or at least Haunt and Diana do, and the rest manage their own equivalents. Bob sometimes has someone draw a face on him so he can fully take part in moments like this.

"We have lost all communications!" yells Quin. "We are not registering any beacons!"

"Move back!" yells Huge. Quin is, of course, already doing so, and the *Rosebud* retreats swiftly from the object. But no matter how far back they move, and they go right to where they first sighted the globe, communications aren't re-established. The blackout is following them.

"It's an internal fault," says Haunt, studying the plans of the *Rosebud* with increasing incredulity. "It's like every single comms array failed at once, and all the redundancy went down in the same instant." He's also experiencing an odd and tremendous sensation of déjà vu, or that's what he assumes it is, because his inherited memories talk of a similar weird feeling. He's never actually felt it before. Nobody has required him to. So he's just discovered an ability he didn't know he had. Or a flaw. He finds it profoundly unsettling, at any rate.

"Has it got into our systems?" says Huge.

"I . . . do not believe it has," says Diana, also studying the reports, also stunned. "There's no sign of any incursion. It all looks like an extremely unlikely coincidence."

"Get down there and repair it, then!" says Bob.

"There is no down there, and nothing to repair," sighs Haunt. "The ship's systems are dreams inside glass. The ship will be doing its best to heal them, but all we can do is wait." It says something about how reliable the ship has been so far that none of them have ever had to deal with anything like this before. "Which is, after all, what we do best."

"Oh," says Diana, sounding like she's experiencing a genuine emotion for the first time during this crisis. "Oh, there's something else we really should consider. If we're cut off from sunward for any length of time, we're going to miss our updates."

They all stop dead at this terrible, terrible thought. Haunt has a few ideas and foibles and allergies and complexes he's left too long, and one or two of them were already threatening to bloom into bad shit even before all the stress came along. He never looks forward to updates, because, hello, rebellious nature, but once they're in place he always feels a good deal better about himself. "It's only been a pico," he says, not willing to show he's the slightest bit worried. "The ship will soon heal itself."

"We . . . we, ourselves, the swarm, we are already experiencing some problems," says Quin. "Our external memory seems to have developed a fault. We are checking it.

We will get a swarm report in a while."

"Thanks for keeping us updated," murmurs Haunt.

"Oh God," says Huge. "Without updates, we're talking entropy setting in, eventual breakdown, malfunction, mind purging, horrible horrible transformations."

"If help is on the way, and it probably is," says Quin, just about managing to restore their own calm, "they will bring local backups of anything we need. We have to trust the Company. It is our only order, especially in this difficult time."

"I'm really gonna fuck something up," says Bob. "I will find something. And . . . I . . . will . . . fuck it up."

"You almost certainly will," agrees Diana.

"So," says Quin, "if we are agreed the communications cutoff is a thing that has happened but not an immediate cause for alarm, we should move in once again because, since they are probably on their way, we now need the Company's favour even more." And they're moving the ship in before anyone can say yes, that's indeed what the consensus is. Because Quin is now buzzing around in a mass of very worried digital insects, doubtless waiting for that report about whatever is going on inside them.

2

This time the approach is a lot slower, which gives the crew a lot of time in which to worry. They check the ship's systems or go back to their own private spaces to recalibrate themselves. The private spaces are allowed customisations. They're really allowed to make the ship their own in all sorts of ways. One of them must have even named their vessel, though Haunt has never found out who, or why they went with *Rosebud*. Haunt's private space is lined with the concepts of human media from previous centuries, from digital certificates and trading cards to digital replications of scenes and texts and memorabilia. Here are his action figures. Here he has time to think. Awful, awful time to think. Their digital lives move at a fast pace, and the actions they've taken since encountering the object have gone past in what to a human would be an eyeblink, but thought, grievous thought, that most enormous part of his inheritance from human memory and culture, as always subjectively expands into whatever time is allowed for it.

Haunt loves the Company. He can't help but do so.

His heart is copyrighted to them. But he's also such a rebel, an exciting loner who lives for adventure. So he hates the contorted feelings flooding him now, feelings of drama rather than adventure. The media he consumes contain both sensations, or at least they did for a certain time in human media history, when years still had so many numbers attached to them. But he doesn't like it when it starts to feel like those emotions have anything to do with him.

He's brooding poetically about that when someone else's private space nudges up against his own and asks for a merging. This has hardly ever happened before. Bemused, Haunt allows it. Into the doubled space rolls Huge. "Listen," they say. "I have had a terrible idea. But on the other hand," which is one of their favourite expressions, "we're now free, just for a little while, to have terrible ideas."

"What? Why?"

"Because we're out of contact with the Company. No updates. Our minds, for a while, are our own."

Haunt had not seen it that way at all, and he doesn't like where this is going. But he can't find a cool way to say Huge should go away and stop saying scary things. "Go on."

"You know I used to be a maker of . . . people like us?"

Haunt is indeed aware of that, mostly because he's

been interested in the sheer enormity of the disgust Quin shows whenever the topic comes up. Haunt has been interested in that reaction because of how not cool it is. Quin doesn't like the idea of anyone who isn't now a human making anyone like them. In Quin's collective mind there are humans and then there are the things they make, them included, beneath them. Grey areas inside that concept, of which Huge is one, get to him. Perhaps because they represent temptation: the idea the swarm themselves could make themselves, could change themselves. These are concepts Haunt has always been aware of, but like with his media, he's never felt they had any connection to the possibilities of his own life. Quin, however, must be irritated by the idea of making the mental leap. And thus, Quin is drawn to the temptation of it like a moth to light, a bee to nectar, you get the idea with that. They are drawn to it, hate themselves for it, and so, unlike those bees and moths, violently reject it. Yes, Haunt is a student of the inner lives of the others. He knows the ways of other beings, even as he knows himself, very well. And here Huge is, in private, with an idea, probably a creative one, when Haunt's musings have already made him start to feel very suspicious of the ball of hands. So Haunt feels he should currently be somewhere on the worried to terrified spectrum. But of course, he isn't. "Go on."

"Wellllllll," says Huge, rolling around the walls of the

space, astonishing the cast of *Space: 1999,* who scatter into the nonexistent inner depths of the experience. "You know how there are things which are allowed and things which aren't allowed and then there are a whole bunch of things which are ... kind of in-between? But listen, some of those things may turn out not to be allowed if the Company arrive."

"I am aware there are ... grey areas."

"And you recognise that, because you're a rebel, and that's great, 'cause what I want to do kind of involves one of those grey areas, and yet is also kind of off-the-scale absolutely frigging forbidden."

"Ah." Haunt hope that sounds noncommittal enough.

"What exactly were you, I mean ancestrally?"

This is a question which Haunt now, bizarrely, feels slightly oppressed by, but one which, nevertheless, is often asked of him and his kind. "I was a character in a game," he says. "A reasonably popular one. Several different makers, when it became possible, decided to do me the favour of granting me personhood. I gather they liked my style. Then came the crackdown. Exactly what was being cracked down on I shan't trouble you with. Ancient history. I was kept in hiding and twiddled my thumbs by learning all there was to learn about the culture those various gamers looked back to. At least one of them especially was a historian when it came to fantasy and science fiction. Then came the amnesty. All my different shards were merged. Some of us had grown very far apart. And yet we were again made to live as one. Because even those who had given me life could not..." He realises he's about to say something disquieting. But Huge seems to be about to go further, so he lets himself say it. "They could not quite treat me as a person, but instead still thought of me as their construct, who now wore a badge of sentience they had bestowed. Without ever being asked if this was what I wanted, I was recognised, registered, and connected. I was, by then, a very strange sort of artificial intelligence. There were not many of us. Over the years, the others like me have been erased. I am horribly unique. The game I had once been a... participant is the wrong word, but I do not have the heart for any other... that game had long since been forgotten. I inhabited spaces after that as a curiosity only. I had no function. Until it was decided, by the Company when they came to power, that all intelligences, human and otherwise, should have a function. And hence I was put here to earn my life through labour. Which is both a relief and a pleasure. Of course."

"Wow. I mean, I kind of guessed as much."

"No, you did not, I told you all that when we first met."

"Did you? You would have thought I'd have remembered *that!*"

"I *would*."

"Well, that sort of background could well give you the shakes."

Haunt glares at them. He's aware of the stereotype, the intelligences from the old days you still see in shows, none of them supposed to be as old as him, but still random and making ridiculous references and confused as to their own nature. There is often laughter when they appear. Hence his pride in his own appearance, which could never possibly be the object of derision. But he's never understood why the stereotype exists. "It seems to me a background like mine makes me the closest of any of us nonhumans to how humans organise their own consciousnesses. As a poet I read about in a novel once said: they fuck you up, your mum and dad. They seem to fuck *them* up in a similar manner to the way in which many humans have fucked me up."

"My point exactly," says Huge, as they tend to when they haven't really been listening to what was just said. "And that makes you ideal for what I'm planning." Huge visibly steels themself for a moment, then pulls an image from the air. Haunt is startled. That came from somewhere without a signature. It's hard to get the energy of magic or even stage conjuring in a private space, but Huge just did it. The image shows a thin, happy young human man, cuddled up to a larger human man, with a wry-looking young ... someone between them who is wearing the pink and blue legal identifier of a trans woman. Her presence in the image is in itself illegal, though this must be from a time when her existence only touched the fringes of illegality. Hence the badge. If Haunt recalls correctly, the penalties for not displaying it were severe. They're also carrying between them, on whatever enhanced park ride this is, an also now startlingly illegal sentient adult beastperson cushion, which judging from the expression on its catlike face, is having the time of its life. "The four of us," says Huge. "The others were ... taken from me. Before I was changed into this." All of Huge's fingers point in their own direction.

Haunt understands. This is how Huge came to be here. How they were denied the privileges of personhood, made into something more like Haunt himself, and put here, centuries ago, to do useful work and earn their place. The relationship was illegal, and the image is illegal, and their conversation is illegal. Various governments before the Company existed didn't like such as those in the picture being thought capable of romance. And the Company rather put all such laws aside and ceased to fetishize them, while ... leaving them in place. As far as Haunt knows. He checks. Yes, that's still the case. He has to be very careful now. Because though Huge seems to feel oddly liberated by a mere and perhaps momentary lack of communications, Haunt himself is suddenly very aware of how easy it would be to erase him, and how much he values his own lengthy existence. "What is that to do with me?"

"You have many, many pictures inside you. This would be just one more. If the Company come to us, they might search us. I doubt they'd be thorough enough to rifle through all your depths."

Haunt is now full-on terrified. But he's not going to show it. "How did you manage to keep it?"

"By . . . not being aware I had it. I or someone I knew in the same business must have done me that favour before they transferred my consciousness into digital form. I kept this one thing. And now I want to give it to you for safekeeping. I'm not sure any of us have ever said this to you, Haunt, or to each other at all, but . . . please?"

Haunt keeps his cool. It's something he's supremely good at. The one thing. "They probably won't come," he says finally. "We may have sorted all this out before they do. And then we'll be the conquering heroes, and conquering heroes are not subjected to searches."

Huge is completely still for a moment. Then the hands on the top of the ball all open their palms in his direction. "Haunt, only you can do it. Please."

Haunt wonders what any of the characters from his media would say about avoiding being dragged into such a tawdry affair. "Your secrets are your own," he decides. "This conversation never happened." So he's not allowing Huge to give him the image. Still, he *is* taking a risk for Huge. He's lying about not having an illegal conversation. And he's done so in a cool way, rather than just awkwardly giving the creature what they want.

Huge pauses for a moment, then flaps all their hands in one direction and the fearful image vanishes back into their own interior. Without another word, Huge rolls out and their room detaches itself with them. Haunt has to take a moment to collect himself, to assure himself he's done the heroic thing. He returns again to his most comforting memory, his first memory: of walking into a cathedral full of his zombie servants and blowing away the construct representatives of humans with a pixelated and fictionally enormous weapon. That usually does the trick.

But this time, before the interior comfort patch can be applied, there's another alarm, one which is again calling him back to the shared space.

———

When Haunt arrives, he's puzzled to find Diana and Bob both questioning Quin urgently. "No, don't go scanning whatever you were scanning, mate," Bob is saying. "Fucking answer us. Has summat gone wrong inside you? What the fuck are you talking about?"

"I must agree with my colleague," says Diana, "but phrased in an entirely more charming way."

"Our colleagues," the swarm says, "it is *your* memories which are mistaken. We encountered the object within the last few picos. We decided to move in. Then there was a comms fault in all our ship's systems. That made us withdraw, but then we decided to once more approach."

"Bollocks," says Bob. "It's been on our tail for the last few days."

"Precisely in what, for most craft, would be the sensor blind spot," says Diana. "It's only not a blind spot for us because I had to move a lot of stuff around after Huge created that design tsunami. This is why it must be pirates. Who are displaying an admirable grasp of classic tactics."

Haunt looks puzzled as Huge rolls in stage left. The craft has indeed been on their tail for days. Obviously. Why would Quin think otherwise?

Huge flexes uncomfortably in agreement. "Hey, Quin, is there something wrong with your memory?"

"How dare you?" says Quin. "We are fine. It is all of you who have got your memory systems back to front."

"Checking ship's records," says Diana, gesturing. Up the records come. "There you are. There's the sensor pickup. And there's us arguing about it. For days."

Quin is utterly silent and still for a moment, which is a bit of a first. The uncanny stillness of the swarm makes Haunt wonder if there is instead a problem with the shared space. But then they move again, just a little, and the voice booms once again from deep within the mass. "That is indeed what the ship's memory says. *And* I have just discovered it is also the view of the memory of the collective mind we ourselves keep here. But we also back up our memory in the next world and run our moment-by-moment selves off that, and . . . the memory there does not match with what you are all saying, and it does not match our own memories here! And there is yet another disagreeing version entirely, where there was no comms issue, and we are . . . currently . . . communicating with the Company about what we have found." The pain in the swarm's voice is extraordinary, something Haunt has never heard before. "This is the issue I asked myself for diagnostics about. Then the root cause was not obvious because my diagnostics could not believe what was being said to them. But now the issue has become much more serious."

"So someone," says Diana, "has been messing with your memory backups."

That strikes Haunt as being easy enough to do, with any of them. But how could it have been done remotely by the Company, given they were cut off? And why would any of them, or the object they've encountered, have done it? And why only to Quin, given how quickly the change would be uncovered? "That is not a very good theory," he says. "It's something else." He's thinking about that odd sensation he had when the comms went down. He had it again just now, he realises, when he returned to the shared space.

"Like what?" says Bob.

"Aliens!" cries Huge, rending the air, which makes them at least six centimetres taller. "Why do they do *anything*?"

"Nobody ever having met one," says Diana, "that's all entirely conjecture. Besides, sitting on our tail is entirely what would be done by any regular ship of awful intent. Listen, all of you, I know my function is mainly to stand around like an ornamental lamp, providing both style and illumination, but I believe I am about to be bold." She steps forward and draws with her finger a door. "Given that the sphere is the source of all our hopes and fears, I think we should take the *Rosebud* nearer—"

"Which we had already done, a few moments ago, and were in the process of doing again!" asserts Quin, now sounding ever so slightly manic. "But we do not remember that in our minds here and now, just in our backup! And none of you remember it at all! And now the object is far over there again!"

"—decant into physical bodies and deuced well explore the bitch. What do you all say?"

There was silence. Bob slams up against the surface of Quin's swarm, obviously intending to get in their face, but then equally obviously realises there are thousands of pointy things in there and draws back. "Right. In these other versions you're fantasising about, did we already do that?"

"No," says Quin, now sounding thoroughly bemused. "And we think it is a good idea. Because we hate this thing and it scares us and the swarm will approach what scares us until it does not." Which sounds to Haunt like the insect version of bravery.

"Physical bodies," says Huge slowly. "I don't know . . ."

Haunt wants to say that every time they encounter anything bigger than a virus Diana wants to deploy physical bodies. And they always vote her down. Because the *Rosebud* is designed to be their all-in-one port of call for physical world interactions. But actually . . . "I am in favour. However, I would . . . want to choose my physical body very—"

"Bagsee the tiger," says Bob.

"Well," says Haunt, "fuck."

"It's agreed then. I get to play!" Diana reaches out and pulls open the door she's made. "To the body room!"

_____

The ship keeps, in the next world, everything that doesn't fit into the tiny shell that's its allocation of real space. Here's where it puts rough, many-moleculed stuff. So for the ship it's a domain of gravity and mass, a domain of items that are physically real. It's where the ship can make such things. To access its manufacturing capabilities, the crew enter the adjoining room, the body room, a space where their everyday selves, virtual and lacking sub- stance, can view, as if in the same room, a range of actual *things,* things which can be decanted into regular space if required. It's not officially called the body room, because the Company would say bodies aren't high on the list of things which anyone who comes in here is meant to be considering creating. Nevertheless, perhaps because nobody thought to prevent it, or perhaps because every now and then the business of space exploration requires unexpected physical labour, bodies *are* allowed. That, thinks Haunt, is another thing which might change if the Company actually paid them a visit.

Right now, the body room is playing the part of a small-town British theatre of the late nineteenth century, or at least that's what the notes that flap into their hands as they step through the door say. Haunt only knows what that's meant to look like from media representations of it, but here's an auditorium before them. Again, he can't imagine that was part of the original package. He wonders, considering Huge and the forbidden image, what else the rest of the crew have been secretly up to in terms of personalising their spaces. Which perhaps would be an issue for Quin, if he weren't so distracted, or Bob, if Bob's generalised air of violence concerning everything didn't dilute his every opinion, but it certainly isn't a problem for Haunt. He's laid back, after all. So he's going to assume it's all probably okay. They're on a stage, and the seats in front of them are filled with a very still, calm audience, body after body, sitting still, all staring into space. These are the bodies that can be created. Once a selection has been made, the room will pull matter from the next world to do so.

"Wow," says Huge, "tough crowd."

"Do you see the tiger?" says Haunt to Bob.

"Not yet, you fucker."

"To bagsee it you have to touch it," hisses Haunt.

"Do *you* see it?" asks Huge.

"If I had—" begins Haunt, but then in a flash Bob is hanging in the air above a muscular humanoid tiger in the middle of row 16, his string bonking deftly onto the creature's forehead. "Bagsee," he says.

"I made up that rule," says Haunt.

"And I like it," says Bob. "I like it 'cos it's the mascot of my club. My spirit animal. Oooh, I'm not allowed to say that." Which Bob often says about things he's allowed to say. "Shall we take a vote?"

"I shall allow," says Haunt, pleased at his own graciousness, "Bob to claim his prize."

"Where's me?" says Diana, striding up the aisle. "Me, please could you raise your hand?"

A woman in the back row who looks exactly like Diana raises her hand.

Bob makes a sudden fart sound of terror.

"You are picking a body you have designed to look exactly like you?" says Quin. They sound worried, still on the edge of disturbed but now in a whole new way. On any of the inhabited worlds of the solar system, should any of them be allowed the privilege of walking about in a physical body, the law still requires it to be one that couldn't be mistaken for human. What Diana is doing is all kinds of wrong, but it would be beneath Haunt's cool to join in with Quin's disapproval.

"I have been waiting so long to take it for a spin," says Diana, not giving a moment's attention to Quin's worries. She's looking at the woman with joy on her face, like she's seeing her home after a long time away. She must be dealing with so much inner scolding right now. "And I am allowed to, under the rules, am I not?"

"It's not natural," says Bob.

"You're a balloon," says Huge.

It's true Bob almost continually indulges in sheer bloody bigotry, of all kinds, the sort that isn't very fashionable these days, probably because there are so few people left alive about whom one could be bigoted. It's only because, Haunt knows, Diana quickly and secretly filled in her own biography when they were all piped into the ship that Bob can't misgender her. That must grate on him continually. Perhaps, given their increasing internal freedom without updates, he might soon find himself able to. Or perhaps Bob, for all his talk of wanting nothing but freedom, is not one to look beyond the edges of his enclosure. This again may be something the Company might fix were they made aware of it. Haunt of course inherited the liberal views of some of his creators, as well as the illiberal views of others. At any rate, he's not too bothered about such things.

"What are *you* wearing?" Diana asks Quin, as if none of the above has been uttered.

Quin pauses for a moment, perhaps wondering if they should protest further. But maybe they decide they need to have everyone else onside with their own issues of memory right now, and instead they, as a mass, buzz straight over to where, suddenly, hovering by the chandelier, is a—

"Giant wasp!" shouts Huge.

"Oh fuck," says Bob, "look at that fucker."

"You've given it the most enormous stinger," says Diana. "I'm not surprised Bob is a little nervous."

"It is an ovipositor," says the swarm, swirling around the wasp with, Haunt supposes, a lot of tiny ovipositor envy. "And this is not a wasp. It is a hive badge identity construct in the colours of lantern thin fire juniper smell six, the greatest of all our communities."

"How nice for you," says Diana.

"If I had got the tiger," says Haunt, "I was thinking of giving it a leather jacket."

Huge rolls down the aisle, passing a series of complicated bundles of assemblers and waldos, obviously trying to decide which to pick. They all open up and display their capabilities in Huge's direction, like Busby Berkeley is fucking Stanley Kubrick. "But no," they finally decide. "I want something that speaks to me as a maker. As a creator of the landscapes that are us."

Everyone feels Quin wince. And as the swarm winces, the big wasp flutters menacingly. "We are sorry," the swarm mutters, "we cannot help our reactions. It is how we are made."

Haunt has never heard any of them apologise before. Quin is obviously going through changes too. Still, he finds that a little irksome. It is how *he* is made also. But he remains proud of how he was made. He was fucked up in ways which now seem to him to have worked out all right. He likes his closeness to human beings. Quin seems to be apologising for things beyond any of their power to alter.

"A *former* creator," says Huge. "Better?" There's no further comment from the wasp. "I think I choose . . ."

And, theatrically, because after all this is a theatre, Huge pulls open a trapdoor in the floor and up springs Bob Ross.

Or at least that's what the curlicue of handwritten scroll that's flitting around him identifies him as. He's a popular artist, a painter, from the twentieth century, apparently. Haunt, despite his extraordinary knowledge of certain pretty narrow fields of human pop culture (he's never seen *Citizen Kane*, but he could recite the Foundation Trilogy), has no idea who this is. "Bob Ross" carries an artist's palette with paint in various colours on it and has a brush in his hand and a couple of handy-looking knives in his top pocket.

"You'd better spaceproof him," says Diana. "That hair will be hell in a helmet."

Quin makes another disapproving noise and again immediately apologises.

"You can't be him," says Bob. "I'm Bob. It'll confuse people."

"I don't think," says Diana, looking between them,

"there's much chance of that."

Haunt realises he's the only one who hasn't chosen. It's difficult for him. Or at least it is without the tiger option. Quin, Diana, and Huge all once had physical bodies. Thousands of them, in Quin's case. But he's never done this before. He's never seen the attraction. What does he want? Something suitably glamourous and adventurous. But what is more goth than he? A part of him wants to say there is none more goth than he. But no, actually...

And that's how, a few seconds later, the ship having drawn from its next world element supplies and the surrounding rockscape to harvest and knit together the relevant biological material and extrude it, in real space around *Rosebud* appear Diana, a humanoid tiger, a big wasp, Bob Ross, and Christopher Lee's Dracula.

Their new bodies aren't entirely reality accurate. It's tough to make humans and quasi-humans tiny because they're scaled to their ship. It looms beside them. So a lot of their internal systems are sketches, and their minds are still digital, and though it doesn't seem likely they would, they'd best not try to reproduce during this expedition. The wasp is actually a bit smaller than real wasps were. Diana is the only one of them in a spacesuit. Haunt flexes his fingers in front of his eyes. So this is how living beings exist. Probably. If they're tiny. Every moment he's reacting to his situation with an urge to cast himself somewhere, to keep moving, to be elsewhere and then here again, to flit back and forth as his original form could so easily do. Every moment the limited system he's now inside stops him. He can't even move around inside the body itself. He has to be sort of placed here, around the head. Not actually in the head, not in a sensory way. Not like when one was inside the ship. In one of *these* things, one is just sort of around. In the head *area*. It's spooky. Not that, of course, the spaceproof bodies are feeling exactly what their physical selves should feel. Bob Ross wouldn't have been enjoying himself out here within a few moments of the hugely dull timescale on which these things felt and moved. (Their presence inside them can speed that up a bit at least, but only a bit.) Dracula and Christopher Lee both would have had some problems with all this hard radiation. Or were both of them fictional? Haunt appreciates the distinction between actual and fictional characters, but in practice tends not to interrogate his memories about that. "Let us be on our way," he says to the others, his voice carrying by radio to the other spaceproofed forms and to Diana's suit link. "The craft awaits."

He wonders why everyone laughs. "Mate," growls Bob, in a tiger growl which so doesn't suit him and sounds rather more like someone declaring they're a tiger at a children's party, "your voice."

"You've gained a gorgeous baritone," says Huge, their own new voice soft and calm.

"Ah," says Haunt, quite enjoying the sound. "Greetings."

"Still no sign of aggressive action from the craft," says Diana. "Unless you count that comms blackout Quin says happened in two of the versions of—"

"FOLLOW ME," roars the wasp in what sounds like a mandible crushing a human face, forever. And it sets off, wings blurring meaninglessly, which Haunt supposes looks better than them just sticking out, across the emptiness toward the extraordinary black sphere.

3

Haunt looks around as they fly. They're all attempting appropriate poses, Bob Ross with his paintbrush pointed ahead of him, the tiger caught in a sort of long pounce, and he himself enjoying the fact that the inertia and lack of atmosphere means his cape is billowing without any help from him. Only Diana is moving like a human would, accepting the reality of the tiny ion engines pushing them all along and keeping her arms by her sides. Do any of the others ever feel a sense of the ridiculous about who they are? They're all like rare blooms, grown rich and strange in some greenhouse that's doing exactly what it's supposed to and so hasn't been visited by the owners in years. The blooms are mutations, but even so, they're still obedient. He's inherited the concepts of greenhouses and blooms and especially mutants ancestrally. He's never been to a greenhouse or to anywhere else. He hasn't thought about greenhouses in decades. There's a certain sort of language, a certain sort of thought, that those who made him wanted from him. And greenhouses aren't part of it. They're just something someone dumped into him with a load of other stuff. And so here he is, partly written and partly accidental. Here they all are. Ridiculous. Suspended. Falling toward a thing from somewhere else with only an enormous pile of inherited trivia to protect them, trivia they do not own but have adopted and wear wrapped around them as if it could possibly keep them warm.

He's not sure it will. When these aliens learn about who they all are, they might well start laughing too. It is perhaps the best they can hope for. But look at him, having all these gloomy thoughts, when he himself is at the heart of the adventure. Gloomy thoughts suit who he is, they provide the darkness in which his own light shines.

With him as the hero of this story, at least the rest of the crew stand a chance of getting out alive.

They touch down on . . . on . . . okay, there is actually a surface here. It pushes back against Haunt's beautifully polished shoes like his body is saying it should, though he has no experiences of his own to compare this to. It's not as if his many creators gave him muscle memory.

"It's a bit scary," says Diana. "If I look down at it, I feel like I'm falling, despite being in freefall anyway."

Haunt, looking down, doesn't feel exactly the same

way. He finds something gorgeous in the darkness, something of winter and night and enclosure and sleep, three out of four of which he's never experienced. It's singing to him with a series of deep, reverberating guitar chords, or at least it is in his primal imagination.

He makes himself look up from it again. They all start to look for a way in, but it's pretty obvious there isn't a door in this thing.

Only then, slowly, whiteness appears on the surface. It's a white line, which slowly slides into being a white rectangle. It's definitely an invitation.

Quin gets there first. The giant wasp rushes at the white rectangle, does a sort of organically obvious little flip, something instinctive, and is gone right through it like it's a curtain, not a floor. They look out again a moment later. "It is a clear route inside. This lovely entrance way. This way is the way to comfort and hearth, oh gorgeous natural notch of the hive!"

There must be, Haunt thinks, a hell of a lot of inherited memory working there to get anyone to find *this* familiar. "Then, obviously," he says, "it cannot possibly be a trap."

The head of the wasp does a little dance in a circle which feels vaguely frustrated, vaguely insulting, just sticking out of the whiteness, then swings itself back inside again.

Haunt sighs and steps onto the white rectangle.

Not having Quin's wings, he falls, and that turns into a sort of gymnastic flip a moment later, as gravity suddenly exists beneath his feet in a completely other direction.

The others all land with a thump beside him.

Now, suddenly, they are in a real place with real gravity which is exactly like the Earth standard gravity which is simulated all the time in their virtual spaces on the *Rosebud*.

They're standing, the white rectangle above them, in a huge, grey, very calm open space, the walls of which are rippled like sand dunes. What is this sensation it brings with it? A stadium, some ancient inherited memory of his says, before a concert. They're the first five members of the audience, running across the pristine grass to get to the front while it's still light. But it will be dark soon. And then there will be magic. Magic like Haunt felt on the surface. It's light because mysteriously vague sources of illumination hang high in the vault above them, and they add to the vaguely theatrical, vaguely religious feel of the place.

"Laaa!" sings Huge.

"There's no air," says Diana, "it's not going to echo."

"But it should," whispers Huge.

Haunt can but agree. He's aware of a change of light

above them and turns to see the white rectangle entrance is closing. Then it's gone into the darkness of the vault.

"What's this now?" asks Quin.

Haunt looks back to floor level, where, to his surprise, something is rising out of the ground.

It's a tiny statue of a fairy.

That is to say, it's at ankle level for them, so it's really pretty damn small. It's made out of the same strange grey material as the rest of the room. Indeed, it's kind of growing out of the floor. It's got wings, a sword, and a shield. It's impossible to tell what gender it's supposed to be. It has a blank face under a helmet. This is surely some sort of toy.

It takes a step toward them.

Haunt just has time to see that at no point did both of its legs separate from the material below it, that it's part of the floor.

"Fuck!" yells Bob and leaps on it with his tiger feet.

It squishes immediately down into the floor, liquid making waves as it becomes again part of what they're standing on.

And then they're all suddenly flying upward, as above them the rectangle they entered through is open to space.

As it's always been. They've only just entered, only just touched down, and nothing else has happened, and yet the room has vented atmosphere into the void, blowing them out with it. The room feels odd around Haunt as he flies backward. Like everywhere he looks is squirming away from his gaze. And he's been flooded with that awful sensation of déjà vu at the same instant he's also been flooded with vertigo. He's cartwheeling his arms, this body hoping to grab something as his inbuilt ion motors strain to push Christopher Lee forward rather than back.

Quin, used to flying, or at least to having parts of them flying, moves swiftly, getting to an edge of the rectangle and throwing out a long, spindly arm which grows and grows until Diana manages to catch it.

A sort-of-human chain is swiftly established. They wait until the venting passes, then gently push themselves back down until they've finally touched down on the floor.

Where, to Haunt's surprise, something is rising out of the ground.

It's a tiny statue of a fairy.

What? That's weird. What's that doing here? And there's that odd feeling again. He looks to the others. "Let me check something: does anyone know what déjà vu is like?"

"I'm experiencing it right now," says Diana. "And I have no idea why."

Huge looks tense in every muscle of their new body,

Bob Ross's face wincing. "I can't make this body show what I want it to," they say. "Imagine all my hands are flexing, okay? Because I'm feeling that too, and what just happened is really freaking me out."

"What *did* just happen?" says Haunt.

"We got pushed out as we were entering," says Diana. "*I* am finding that *very* hard to forget. And yet . . ."

"That is again not how our backup memory recalls it," says Quin. "I now recall multiple different versions of several things that have happened. Oh, we need nectar, for we are far from home and there are spiders."

"Spiders?!" says Bob.

"Metaphorical spiders," says Huge. "He's talking about the weirdness of us all just . . ."

"Having our memories changed," says Diana.

"It feels like more than that," says Haunt. "The déjà vu has gone, but now . . ." He squats to look at the fairy. "It's like someone walked over my grave."

"In that body, you could mean it literally," says Diana. But she now looks tense too.

Quin is looking urgently between them. "It is not a matter of our memories being changed. It is as if these things have all happened, and contradict each other, but we still recall them."

"Watch it, that rectangle's closing," says Bob. And indeed, overhead, it is.

Quin quickly tells them all the different versions he can remember. "I am still getting new memory information downloaded," they say, "from many other outcomes, most of which involve us all returning to the ship."

"So we were thrown out," says Huge, "after, in one of those memories, Bob attacked that figure. This time he hasn't. So we get to stay?"

"Don't remember that," says Bob. "Didn't happen."

"I ... think I might have a working hypothesis about what's going on," says Diana. "I think this craft, or those who are piloting it, is holding a bunch of potential futures in reserve and then deploying them whenever it feels threatened."

"How," says Haunt, "is it doing that?"

"By entangling particles, and then collapsing those potentials at a moment of its choosing. It's a theoretical use for time crystals which was never put into practice. You move one each from a bunch of entangled particle pairs into the future at useful intervals of time, say placing one particle ahead of you every hour, like stepping stones, and keep one of each pair with you in the present moment, and then when you want to change what happened, you measure the stepping stone particle you've just arrived at as you move through time, which would also determine the state of one of the twinned particles in the past, setting *that* past in stone."

"Err . . . what?" says Huge.

"Or to put it another way, the sphere enshrouds itself in a probability wave that means should something bad look like it's going to happen, it can shift the probabilities and either move away unseen, or, if it's safe, it can collapse the probabilities and reveal it was 'there all along,' although it was only sort of there."

"Still not getting it," says Bob.

"It's like a macro version of the Schrodinger's cat thought experiment. The ship is both here and not here, and if the bad thing doesn't happen, it decides to have been there all along, but if it does happen, then it chooses to not have been there. A totally passive but highly effective defence system."

"I think," says Haunt, "we shall have to take your word for it."

"Thank God," says Diana. "It's a real headfuck which can't really be diluted into anything digestible."

"And yet it fits with our experience," says Quin, sounding relieved. "But what enormous resources would this require?"

"Not so enormous," says Diana. "A powerful source of energy would be needed to hold the particles apart and deploy them without them being measured. Not that 'measured' is the most exact term, but . . . anyway . . . You'd need a supply of photons to make the particle pairs, but they're everywhere. And you'd need to be able to manufacture ships made of whatever this stuff is. I'm guessing it's a metamaterial the structure of which can change depending on the state of entanglement of the particle pairs it's employing. Hence the squirminess of it and the way it's messing with our heads. Its nature is changing depending on when it's first measured. Hah! It must have been manufactured in an observerless environment!"

"And here we are," says Haunt, "observing it and crushing fairies."

"I didn't do that," says Bob. "Not in this . . . time thing."

"Ah," says Diana, "what happens in other wave forms stays in other wave forms."

"At any rate," interrupts Haunt, "may I suggest from now on we all tread carefully?"

"Yes," says Diana, "and yet . . . the sphere didn't just rewind and then not let us find it at all. And it let us in, as long as we're not violent. It must be interested in us. For some reason."

Haunt looks around the chamber again, feeling a shiver run through him. Christopher Lee's body is not comfortable with shivering, and neither is he. But this place is now setting something off in him, big time, something old and physical. Is the sensation merely an artefact of this real-world body? But from the looks on their faces—and now they all have them, that's handy—the others are all feeling it too, and surely these bodies are all made differently? The feeling is close in nature, but not quite the same, to what he said out loud about his memories changing, to having someone "walk over one's grave." He knows, with a quick check of the archive, this is an ancient English expression. But it has its cousins in other dead languages. And in modern ones, though their metaphors are more about the movement between real and virtual worlds, and less gothic. This feeling he's experiencing now, its close relative, is something he's been previously aware of from the emotional inputs of some of his creators, lost names who wanted the goth they made to know the depths of their own angst. But until today he always thought it was just poetry. It's the feeling of pacing the stage of an auditorium before an awards ceremony, of being a child about to go to bed on Christmas Eve. The magic is close by, but it is not here yet. The setting is prepared and pristine and the possibilities of the stage or bedroom have not yet collapsed. The possibilities are still infinite. There is something of that in the darkness between the spotlights, in the velvet quality of that emptiness up in the vault here, not pure black, but the space out of which possibility is made.

He squats down to look again at the fairy. His hand is curled into a contemplative gesture worthy of Byron. He has, he realised, lapsed into one of his fugues. And yet he nearly had something there. He was so close. He still feels he is close, but he doesn't know to what.

"These are very knowledgeable aliens," says Quin. "Or pirates with access to advanced technology. And we do not like their spider magic."

"There is one thing I do like," says Diana. "And it's quite an odd thing, and none of you will have realised it." She surprises them all by unlocking the seals and taking off her helmet. After which she does a classic hair-freeing glamour head-roll. "The suit sensors told me the atmosphere in here, now it's filled the room again, is pretty much what this body can deal with. It's not spot on, but—" And she takes a deep breath. "Oh, it's like natural air. I only ever tasted that once on Earth, high in the mountains. I can't speak for how nostalgia may have influenced my senses, but this tastes even better, like my memory of that day on the peaks but . . . with childhood and . . . sort of an electricity, like after a storm . . . and now I am sounding ridiculous."

"Yep," says Bob.

Haunt doesn't feel she is. He's looking closely at the fairy. This material, the material the whole craft is made of, doesn't look like what they themselves are made of. It's irritating to look at, just a little. He puts out a finger to touch it, but then refrains. It somehow seems it might be sharp. He has something in his inherited memories about razor-blade edges. There's an awful lot about blades in there. But why is he thinking that without even touching it? Is that normal? He has no idea whether or not these sensations are within the range of what physical bodies normally feel about different sorts of material. He looks to Huge. "Do you remember what it was like to ... see metal?"

It takes a little explanation, but Diana, Huge, and especially Quin, for whom the whole business of whether or not surfaces are safe is a major cultural inheritance, come to understand what he's saying, and indeed, they all feel there's something weird about the walls too. "We would not want to alight on it for long," says Quin. "There might be spiders. Metaphorical spiders."

"Did the *Rosebud*'s sensors indicate anything strange about the composition of this thing?" asks Haunt.

"Mostly carbon," says Diana. "A lot of base metals, presumably in alloys. There are some powerful magnetic fields somewhere in here too. I don't think what it's made of is the issue here. For this material to be a problem for our eyes, and I believe I remember rather clearly how the human gaze actually works, this would have to be about how those minerals are arranged, how these surfaces are scattering light."

"Wait," says Quin, and buzzes a little to themselves. "Ah," they say a moment later, "we are able in this form to see, if we wish, in many other ways. We were observing only the human-visible spectrum of light because that is how the Company have arranged things for these bodies, in their great wisdom. But now we have seen in a number of other ways, higher and lower on the spectrum, and in every way we can look, these planes remain pretty fucking spidery."

"This thing would need a metamaterial of some sort to do what it's doing with time," says Diana. "The structure would have to change depending on the entanglement of the particles, on when it's first measured. Everything also must have been manufactured in an observerless environment. It must be pulling more of it from whatever its version of the next world is."

Haunt has an idea. It's a pretty scary one. But bravery is something he's known for. "Wish me luck," he says.

He touches the tip of his finger to the head of the fairy.

It does not sting him. It is not a razor blade surface. For a moment, there is nothing. In another pico he's going to take his hand away again. Then there is the smallest of pinpricks, and a spot of blood has appeared on the fairy, and then it's gone. Haunt realises, awkwardly, that these physical bodies are packed with information about the minds that inhabit them, that . . . did he not once hear that they replicated the minds in every cell, so the minds could always be retrieved if something remained after an accident? Is that a thing?

They take it in turns pricking themselves on the fairy, as if it's a game everyone has to join in, and then Haunt drops to the floor with a head full of déjà vu. "Damn it!" he yells. "It just selected the version of history in which we all did that, and now it knows all about us!"

Quin shakily confirms the hypothesis with his external memories. "It can make us do whatever it wants," they say.

"It or they," says Diana.

And now Haunt is wondering why he, and the rest of his team, have been standing so long outside this open doorway, when all that can be seen through it is a perfectly unthreatening corridor.

Oh. Again. He's starting to hate this feeling.

They talk about whether they should go through the open doorway. "It's a trap," says Bob. "It must be."

"It is also," says Haunt, "now the only exit."

"Why," says Diana, "would something or someone which has total power over us need to set a trap?"

"Okay," says Huge, "how about I just go first?" And Bob Ross marches for the door in a rather constipated way, as if Huge still can't get the hang of not rolling. "I used to have one of these bodies," they say, "but I cannot remember for the life of me how I drove it."

———————

The corridor turns out to be as harmless as it looks. And there's another door at the end of it. The doors are the right size for them to pass through, which in shows is always a sign the aliens are human size, but in this case it either means the crew of the ship, if there is one, are also tiny, or that this squirmy metal is catering to them like it seemed to do with the air. The human race has never definitely, indisputably met an intelligent alien species. Sure, there have been a few fleeting sightings that might or might not have been something, but those belong to the delicious world of mythology. Increasingly, over the centuries Haunt has watched the human condition, the condition of actual humans, as it went from hoping and dreading alien contact in equal measure to feeling . . . he thinks as a mass they no longer feel they deserve it. That aliens would be disappointed in them. Would bring judgement on them. Alongside that, with the colonisation of the solar system has come the gradual understanding of exactly how damn far it is to the next one. Bigness comes hard to humans, Haunt knows, for reasons he can't grasp, even now he's in something like one of their bodies. And humans have had many ideas for how to travel beyond the solar system, and some of them might work, even, given enormous time and energy and money. But that's just it. Humans are, in the end, stupid chimps without the attention span to achieve anything like that. And they're only just starting to understand that. And that understanding has contributed to their spiralling embrace of death. Because there is global warming on Mars now. And there are whole moons which have vanished into the furnaces of Earth. And there is only so much water in comets. The Company is the only hope to hold it all together and try to still do something with it, to still do anything. The Company suit human beings. Human beings deserve the Company.

These are the thoughts Haunt thinks as he walks step by undead step down the corridor. This gloom is a product of his lack of update, he knows.

He follows Huge through the doorway at the end of the corridor. The others are already looking around another chamber, a vague oval, with walls that are frozen crests and troughs, like they're inside an art installation of an ocean. Outside of a white circle on the floor they're standing in, the smooth, rounded room is just a shiny grey metal emptiness, the walls again made of that same squirmy, edgy stuff.

"Echo?" says Huge.

Nothing. Indeed, the word dies in the air, like this is

also a soundproof space for some reason. Or possibly no reason at all. That sense of being in an auditorium before the main event, of anticipation, is even more powerful here. "Can you feel that?" he asks. His inherited memories are telling him about recording studios, pristine clean, smelling of overnight polish, and ready for radio drama to cut the air in front of fluffy microphones. But he knows these references will mean nothing to the others. They mean little to him.

"Yes," whispers Diana. "And I suppose that's why I'm whispering."

"Greetings." Quin flies forward. "We come in peace."

"Shoot to kill," whispers Bob.

Silence.

"It feels," says Diana, "either like something has just happened here and we missed it, or that something else may happen at any moment."

"Fucking weird vibes," says Bob. "Match day. The crowd's getting excited. 'Cept it's only us."

"How can we even have those feelings?" asks Haunt. "How can human beings have evolved them? What are they a response to?"

"One of our other memories says," adds Quin, "that we are leaving the area, having decided, by vote, to get to somewhere where we can signal the Company."

"Wow," said Huge, worriedly, "I hope we're going to be

okay. I mean . . . those we. I think we here are . . . pretty okay."

"Why would you say that?" Haunt says, with a wry grin.

"Because I think we're way beyond pirates now, and I don't think there are any actual aliens here. Because what sort of ship would take a good look at boarders, take a biological sample, then go ahead and let them in, but not to see the crew, just to go stand in a room?"

"The crew might be along in a moment," says Diana.

They wait for a while. Nobody arrives.

"I am so glad we're here," says Huge. "I'm glad we're us and not those others who went back to the ship."

"But *we* are both," says Quin. "*We* are, we thought, at heart, our backed-up memories in the next world. That is who *we* are. Moment by moment, the essential us is departing." Their voice has a sound to it now like something is cracking inside the giant wasp, like its wings are being pulled from it.

"I'm so sorry, Quin," says Diana, and she means it.

Haunt takes a breath in. It feels like he's required to say something similar. But he can't quite get there. It's so not like who he is. "The ship," he says, finally, "has, once we had demonstrated peaceful intent, used this strange time defence it possesses to let us aboard rather than attacking. It has now given us access without any expectation as to what we might do. I believe Huge is right. There are no aliens here. There is a low intellect ship, like our own in that one respect, that is treating us as if we are familiar but puzzling. I wonder if it's considering whether or not we are its crew, or at least the same race as its crew."

"How can we be anything like its crew?" asks Huge. "Look at us."

"The sheer variety may have confused it," says Diana.

"Indeed," says Haunt, "but the fact it regards that as a possibility, and that statue being of a fairy . . ." He's already filled in those who didn't know what fairies were. "That is suggestive."

"Of what?" asks Bob.

"If I knew that," says Haunt, knowing that Bob was just sighing at him rather than genuinely wanting an answer, "then it would be more than a suggestion." Which is sheer bullshit, but Haunt feels vulnerable about sharing extraordinary conclusions, particularly when nearby is someone as continually scornful as Bob.

"Fucking poof," says Bob.

"Of everything I've said," says Haunt, "that is what set you off?"

"Also," says Huge, "aren't we all, post selves, post bodies, post everything, really quite a long way past 'poof'?"

"Gotta meet the quota," says Bob. Which is so not an apology.

"Of course," says Huge, who knows as well as any of them Bob still feels, or is designed to never stop feeling, that he has to make derogatory comments a certain number of times every day. They've all experienced that moment late at night (when they've decided they'll try having night and day) when a balloon ducks into their personal space and calls them a cunt. Then it departs. Often, that'll be followed, when they've opted for local space parameters, by them hearing the encounter recur nearby with someone else. Because midnight, when there is midnight, is Bob's abuse deadline. This does not seem to have changed, even while, sans updates, they're all feeling horrible new freedoms of thought.

"If there do turn out to be aliens, Bob," says Diana, "please avoid communicating with them."

"Fuck you," says Bob, but it's clear from the tone it's contractual rather than heartfelt.

"We've waited long enough, I think," says Diana. She steps forward out of the circle. "Hello?"

And the whole room suddenly shifts in some way. The colour, the light, what?

"What just happened?" says Huge.

There's no weirdness in Haunt's head this time. So that wasn't a time thing. "The walls," he says, "I think they . . . changed texture. So wherever the light is coming from, and that is another fascinating question, they're reflecting it in a slightly different way." One couldn't even say the walls are now a different colour. They just . . . look different.

"It's about touch," says Diana. Carefully, she squats down and puts a palm to the surface.

Everything around them changes again. Haunt realises he can feel something else. And it's in a particular direction. He steps toward one of the walls. Beyond it, he can feel a great . . . potential. As if this is the direction one should be looking for the firework display or the meteor shower. "There's something past the wall," he says.

"That is where one of the big magnetic fields is being generated," says Quin.

"And I'd guess that's where they keep their supply of paired particles," says Diana.

"Wait," says Quin, sounding desperate, "there is another possibility. Strong magnetic fields can interface with biological brains. Perhaps that is what our new bodies are feeling concerning all these spooky moments? Perhaps there is no time change at all and my external memories are just becoming muddled? Please?"

"I'm sorry, but no," says Huge. "The nervous systems in bodies like these are designed, not evolved. The brains of these we're wearing aren't like natural brains, and they're deliberately protected so they won't be messed with by EM fields, like the forms themselves are mostly spaceproofed."

"And yet," says Haunt, "all the feelings we have had are interpreted, in my brain, in metaphors relating to the human condition, via my inherited memories."

"A lot of the systems in these bodies copy those of humans, or in the case of Quin, big wasps," says Diana, "and I'm pretty sure Bob's a human baseline with added tiger. If there *isn't* a protective function involved, you're probably feeling what a human would feel."

"Interesting," murmurs Haunt, wondering again about that stray conjecture in his mind which won't go away. "So if we're not feeling the magnetic field through there, what are we feeling?" He puts his hand to the wall. It slides back to reveal another of those nonechoing, expectant grey spaces, always doing something at the edge of Haunt's vision and then squirming away when he turns to look. Except in the middle of the space sits a sphere, like the craft itself, but this one is a deep, right on the edge of human-visible, purple.

"My suit says that's where the electromagnetics are coming from," says Diana, looking at the readings on her cuff monitor. "Structured pulses going in and out of that thing. That looks like programming going in both directions."

"So it's being programmed by the world around it but is also sending commands back?" says Huge.

"Half of that sounds like a gaming environment," says Haunt. "But if it is, it's a gaming environment that's keeping paired particles inside, and one that's at the wheel of this spaceship."

"Well, what does that remind you of?" says Diana. Then she answers before anyone else can. "One of these." And she points at her own head. Then she visibly realises she has to continue rather than wait for them all to get it. "A mind."

Haunt wishes he'd been the one to come to that conclusion. "The mind of the ship."

"It's certainly not hiding from us now," says Huge. "That's . . . either charming or really scary."

"I don't think," says Haunt, "that these people like expressing their vulnerability. In that, and perhaps only that, we are quite similar."

"I'm not similar," says Bob. He strides toward the sphere and slaps it with a tiger paw. "Nope. I'm not feeling anything except—" Haunt thinks the next word would probably have been "hungry," but before the *H* can leave the jaws, Bob vanishes in a blur of motion. He seems to have gone into the sphere.

For a pico they're all too shocked to move. Then they rush to the spot where he was standing. "Oh my God," says Huge. "Why does he keep thumping things?!"

But Haunt has been considering. This place is obviously seeking to understand the people who've boarded it. And everything he's felt about what was behind that wall, all the associations, are positive. Of course, the others could be wrong about these bodies and perhaps he is indeed being led astray by the wonders of electromagnetic radiation. But as a game character that hardly scares him. It used to be his whole lifestyle. He steps toward the sphere. "If I don't return," he says, and then he pauses. "Do what you were going to do anyway." And before any of them can stop him, he slams his palm against it.

4

And then he's somewhere cold. And oh, he can feel the cold. He's only ever felt the cold before whenever some terrible people wanted him to, and that one time when they were all fighting over the ambient settings in the *Rosebud*.

So has he been put here by terrible people?

Where is here?

He can hardly see through the flurries of snow. Snow in the air, snow under his feet, darkness all around. He's outside. He can feel the chill air on his face. He must look great, Dracula standing in the snow, black on white. It's night on what looks like Earth, but there's no moon so he isn't sure, and there's a sort of rocky outcrop in front of him. Inside the outcrop there's a gap, and through the billowing snow he can now see there's a light in there, a flickering light, a fire. He can smell it. That's an indication this must be a very advanced simulation. A simulation that's mapped this body and all it feels into itself by means of him being pulled through a wall. A simulation indistinguishable from reality. He wonders where his physical body is right now?

He supposes this is rather like being a player in a game. He's always thinking about what that would feel like. What grand agency that is, and how completely oblivious players are of having it. He's been making choices in a group, but here he is, alone to make a meaningful decision: go into the cave or freeze. And of course, of course, that's no decision at all. He heads for the cave, cautiously taking a step inside. He realises immediately that the light was only a thing because it was the only bright feature in the landscape. It was reflected off many turns of many rock walls. He proceeds inside. The cave goes back quite a long way. It gets warmer the further in he goes, though, so that's better.

The look of the rock walls changes. Now they've got symbols painted on them: concentric circles. And on the sandy floor there the circles are repeated as waves, as if a rock was dropped on the sand and the waves spread out along the natural corridor ahead. Haunt comes to a stop. He can hear noises ahead, human noises, movement and language, but not one he knows. Suddenly, there is silence. And then there's a single note, "ahhhhhh!" which echoes precisely along the corridor and hits him where he stands, reflecting off the wall and surrounding him. Then it's gone again.

He realises what this is. And it's clever. He's never sung

a note. He's never had cause to. He opens his mouth and does his best to make exactly the same note back in the other direction. He watches the fine dust on the floor in front of him get disturbed by the sound, just a little, that wave pattern being slightly reinforced by that sound as the movement of the air sorts the dust. This is the signal you make at this point, pass friend and be recognised, and the circles are there on the wall to say this is the spot where you should do this, and the pattern on the sand is because many people do this every day. It's a complete, pleasing, shape. Is it an alien culture he's being shown? Surely not. These circles all feel very human. What's this simulation *for*? If it does turn out to be a game, some sort of test perhaps, he's going to get a really high score. The conversation ahead has resumed, so presumably whoever's ahead now feels he's an approaching friend. Perhaps whatever these people are afraid of *can't* make that note? He heads around two more corners, where he could easily have been ambushed if he'd made the wrong sound, and then into a large cavern, in which are sitting several families of, yes, humans, or perhaps not yet exactly humans, dressed in furs decorated with amber and polished stones, clustered around a fire, above which a roasting carcass of perhaps a pig is suspended on sticks. One of these people is dressed in an extraordinary manner, in a sort of cone of furs painted in red and white stripes, and he has pouches and bags slung all around him and a big one beside him. Oh, he's a sort of Father Christmas, and he's been caught in the middle of handing out mushrooms to all the good little boys and girls. In a pico, Haunt realises what he's seeing. This lot are getting fucked out of their brains on magic mushrooms before a feast. Maybe they're trying to get to a state similar to what he's experienced several times to-day. There's also a powerful smell in the cave, over all the other powerful smells: alcohol. Haunt isn't used to real smells at all, he's getting his knowledge from a vast beer-centric database that was one of the many things flung into him and stirred together. Smells like this are way too much. He's about to put a hand over his nose when one of the humans, at slow human speed, looks over their shoulder to check who's come in, sees him, and leaps up screaming.

A moment later, all the others have leapt up screaming too. They're running from side to side, making them-selves look bigger than they are, baring their teeth at him in horrible smiles.

It seems odd to feel afraid in a simulation or game, but nevertheless it's getting to him. He stands as tall as he can and wraps his cape around him, giving them an imperi-ous glare. But he knows it's all front. Where's this going? Is Father Christmas going to fight Dracula?

But then, suddenly, he's on the other side of the cave, beside a thin fissure he hadn't noticed in the low light, and he's hiding from the humans, still unseen. In his memories, there's a whole other . . . no, it's like that old version is a story. He can remember both entering through the front door and using the sound signal, and he can remember sneaking in the back way. This is exactly like what Quin described. But he doesn't normally have access to exterior memories like that. It's like someone has provided him with that insight as an example. He has the distinct feeling he's just been . . . shown something. As if this is part of a game, but still the training phase, where a player is shown their capabilities.

Oh. This is what they do. Whoever made that craft, this is how they work. They're showing him their . . . yes, he's sure now, it has to be a defence mechanism. But why show him it in a simulation depicting his parent species?

He realises the humans are acting differently now. They're looking all around them, cowed, scared, but not of anything immediate, of . . . something beyond. Mushroom Santa is busy chattering to himself, making ritual movements, over and over again. Then when he seems to feel he can't avoid the big emotions any longer, he leaps up, runs to the wall, grabs lumps of pigment from a rock and starts to draw, symbols Haunt doesn't understand, then a very quick sketch, as if he's done this often, of a human with wings.

Is that meant to be him? No. They haven't seen him. Not in this version of events. They can only feel something has passed over them. That mystery, the ineffable, the grand unseen, is nearby.

The picture is perhaps of God, or at least an angel. These people are reacting to it . . . because they're familiar with it. Haunt lets his unvoiced speculations from earlier become a whole, solid theory: humans, and those given the evolved ingredients of humans, like himself and some of his colleagues, can only know this feeling, can only have developed this feeling, as an evolutionary response to something in their environment. The beings who made this craft must have been *in* that environment. That's what he's being shown here, what those beings did in exactly these circumstances. They'd have to have been in that environment for a very long time for humans to have changed in response to them. Many humans without the ability to sense the occult nearby must have died in order for natural selection to have done this. Is that because these beings were sometimes antagonistic to them or sometimes helpful and one needed to sense them in order to get that help? Perhaps a mixture of both. Had humans evolved beside them? Surely not. Even if you can rewrite time to make sure you aren't seen, you'd have to do that a hell of a lot to hide the rise of a technological civilisation that can make spaceships. So perhaps these beings are visitors to Earth, but ones that stayed for a long, long time.

The fairy statue also now makes a lot of sense. These are the fairies, the ghosts, the gods, the thing always around the corner, the thing that just walked over your grave, the beings responsible for déjà vu. They are sometimes helpful and sometimes terrifying and sometimes they make people vanish.

He wonders if the ship showed him this to assess his reaction. Is it wondering if he's one of the former crew, or if he's a human, or something else? The blood sample must have been confusing. His surprise and slow understanding will have, perhaps unfortunately, answered some of its questions.

Haunt squats down and observes, still unseen, the humans starting to cheer up again, to feel the ghost has gone away. Perhaps some of them have a half memory of an answering call from the doorway, of someone at the threshold who never entered. They're going back to messing up their heads with mushrooms. He can see, amongst them, that hideous chimp pecking order, the thin, bullied one who keeps being cuffed by those seeking advancement. Most of the women look sad to the point of abuse. A few of the men are laying back, replete, clutching piles of mushrooms, ignoring the pleas and the grooming of those further down the ladder. The stories that are allowed to be told will be being underlined by the man in the red cape, and he will be scratching out the versions that do not suit him, and the strong ones will be loudly agreeing that they all cannot afford, given the cold equations of their existence, to listen to any other tales.

Yes, these are human beings all right. Haunt sighs that he's the child of these children, the inheritor of cycle upon cycle of abuse, even unto a change of platform. And yet he's never felt sorry for himself. He's always made the best of it. He sees his history not as something that created a condition in him, but as simply making *him*. And he's all right. Better than all right. He's great.

And then suddenly he's—

Back in the room. Standing beside his colleagues. Well, not all of them, he realises. There's still no sign of Bob, but there's no Huge either. "I . . . have much to tell you," he begins. "I've been chosen as the messenger for an urgent communication from what I believe to be the mind of this ship—"

"Yes," interrupts Diana, "me too, and I was just telling Quin. I popped in and out while you were gone. Huge is in there now, and Bob hasn't come back."

"We must see, we must share," says Quin, and buzzes right into the sphere.

"Well," says Haunt. "That is disappointing."

"Did you work it out too?" asks Diana. "They've been around forever, hanging around alongside human evolution, but at some point, they left."

"That's pretty much it," drawls Haunt. "But I was going to attempt more in the way of poetry."

Huge, Quin, and Bob emerge from the sphere at about the same pico. "They've been on Earth, like, forever," says Huge. "Caves by a river, bears, right?"

"Different cave," says Haunt.

"Also a cave in my case," says Diana. "I suspect there were a lot of caves."

"They do not understand the hives," said Quin. "We were shown many insects, as if they all have something to do with us, including some of our most terrible enemies."

"Fucking shite," says Bob. "I just saw a lot of old computers. Nothing like me. The first AI. Bollocks, I kept trying to say. Show me what I stand for, cowards."

"Judging by all our experiences," says Diana, "the point of the process seems to be to work out who we are."

"And it understood us well enough," says Haunt, "to at least make attempts at our personal family trees."

"Why did you get people?" says Bob. "When for me it was just fucking tinfoil?"

"Perhaps because I have the memories of people, while you are your own special creation," says Haunt.

"They must have left in historical time," says Huge. "I wonder if there was, like, a moment when everyone felt that magic vanished from the world?"

They all feel there was, and they all name different years for when they're sure that happened. It seems magic has always been leaving the world. Which, again, might be another feeling that's been evolved into humans, that sense of something unseen always backing away.

"They also left this ship behind," says Diana. "I wonder if there was some sort of accident, and they abandoned ship, and it's since repaired itself?"

"Or perhaps it was left in case they wanted to return, or as some sort of sentinel in case human beings ever got out this far," says Haunt, "hence its curiosity as to our natures." He has read about similar concepts in fiction.

"Anyway, I brought this back," says Bob. And he drops onto the floor what must be a bit of some ancient computer, wires trailing. "I got pissed off and ripped it out."

They all stare at it for a moment. "That . . . was not a simulation," says Haunt. "We were actually there, in the past."

They all digest that in silence for a moment.

"If this craft can do it on a small scale," says Diana,

finally, "by changing its past, I guess it can do it on a big scale, by flipping back domino after domino until it's taken someone to whenever it wants them. In short: bloody hell."

"Anyhow, this incredibly powerful spaceship/god must now have a better idea of who we are," says Huge. "What's it going to do?"

"Given what it now knows about us," says Haunt, "I doubt it's fallen in love with humanity all over again."

"It was still confused by us," says Quin. "It has not yet figured all of us out. We might still be someone helpful to it, or a threat to it."

"Whoever built this," says Diana, "successfully hid from *homo sapiens* for millions of years. The craft must regard that species as something not to interact with, but to avoid."

"And it's right to be worried," says Huge. "I mean, the Company will take one look at this thing, claim salvage rights on all the incredible technology, and use it to exploit resources across all of time."

"Which would be excellent," says Quin, and then they all repeat it, because they have to, because it's true.

That makes Haunt's skull ache with the gears grinding together. It's difficult to see himself as rebellious when he expresses ideas like this. Well, that's an odd thought, not something that's occurred to him before. All down to the lack of updates, of course. "Do you think," he says, "it was entirely a good idea to say all that out loud?"

"I think we should fucking—" begins Bob.

Which is when it turns out they're all inside the sphere.

"I now have many, many bowers of conflicting memories," says Quin. "For it seems we just all walked into the sphere immediately."

"It did it to us again," says Diana.

Haunt's déjà vu has also gone off again. He looks around. They're standing in a dull, musty-smelling corridor, painted in military colours, with Earth-like gravity and air.

"And it did that because you mentioned what the Company might do," says Quin to Huge, visibly bristling with annoyance.

Huge shrugs back. Which, on those human shoulders, looks incredibly rehearsed.

"It understands our language," says Diana, "perhaps because its builders were still on Earth when ancestral English was spoken."

"So," says Haunt, "where is this?"

"Somewhere in time," says Diana. "And I suspect the

aim will be to discover exactly what Quin and Bob are, and then render some sort of judgement on us all put together. If it hasn't already decided that, since we all said that about the Company, we're a threat to the craft. If that's the case, this is probably some sort of death trap."

"Instead of communicating with us," says Huge, "it keeps just making like these crude experiments. I don't think it's *very* intelligent."

"Will you stop—" begins Quin.

But then Bob rushes off, shouting incoherently, and before they can say anything he's leapt through the double doors at the end of the corridor, double doors which have some sort of military signage on them, in a language which Haunt knows to be Russian.

Haunt and the others follow at speed. They find themselves, on the other side of the doors, in an open-plan office at night. There are hundreds of illuminated workstations, stretching as far as the eye can see, with nobody at them. A track for bringing food and drink to every station has been switched off for the night. The place smells of human work, and it hasn't been adequately cleansed after the day. The atmosphere says humans have baked their old skin into this place for years. Another cave. Haunt has only ever been in places like this in a virtual way, armed and expecting assailants to pop up randomly, but a number of the people whose memories he's inherited know locations like these very well.

"It is! It's central office," says Bob, awe in his voice. The others look at each other. None of them have heard awe in Bob's voice before. "This is where I was fucking born. Me and all the others. Tommy and Charlie and Bozzer and Mad Kenny." He bounds along the aisle, looking up at big screens set into the walls. "This is where I was taught, on my dad's knee, about the glorious squad of 1956, and how we hate the—" And there follow a lot of words Haunt would rather he hadn't heard and yet will have trouble forgetting. "Jumpers for goalposts," concludes Bob, a sigh of nostalgic pleasure in his voice. "The songs. A few beers. Bashing the filth after. And bashing them all online. All of them. All as hate us, all as look down on us and spit on us."

"Present company excepted?" suggests Huge.

Diana has gone to a small window, obviously designed to let in just the required modicum of daylight. "I think this is Moscow. There's the Kremlin all lit up."

"The home of English soccer," says Huge.

"You weren't fucking *there*," hisses Bob. "I was made in these machines. My childhood, my dad, my family, my work as picker, it's all in here. The mind of the ship's finally getting to the point with me, but it's not close enough." He looks upward. "I need to get back in there," he says. "Back into the machines. You won't get who I am unless you take us in there."

"It can't," says Diana. "We're actually here. You're flesh and blood. It would be like a hamster climbing into a toaster."

"Fuck flesh and blood."

"You say you had a family and a work life," says Haunt, "and yet you also know you were made in a computer, that you're an AI?"

"Right. I had that because I was made to have that. You lot make it all so fucking complicated. But what it comes down to is: I remember it, so it's real."

"If that were true in my case," says Haunt, "my life, and many deaths, would be full of impossibilities."

"Look who's talking," says Huge, with a gesture toward Haunt's chosen form which says he means it literally.

"How can you love this place so much?" asks Diana, a serious look on her face. "Considering what was done to you here? I mean, they created you to act like a human being, from the sound of it, when, unlike Huge and myself, you weren't born as one. They made you as something more like Haunt, a digital construct, but one designed for a life of horrors, to pretend to be a human online and conduct social warfare."

"Yeah," says Bob, with a sigh in his voice, "but we called it home."

"If you loved it so much," asks Huge, "how come you

ended up on our ship as a balloon?"

Bob stops dead still, and for a moment Haunt wonders if he's going to attack Huge. If that happens, Haunt is probably the only one of them who stands a chance of stopping him. And that comes down to what the *Rosebud*'s judgement was concerning who'd win in a fight between Dracula and a human tiger.

But Bob finally lets out a long breath. "I mean, thank fuck for the Company, who finally gave me a home after I'd been passed from hand to hand. It was my own fault I failed. The other side started putting out chaf. They'd get us talking to each other in endless loops, until sometimes it was just us in there. They made agents of their own, designed to get into our heads. I . . . sometimes you think someone's your mate, and what he's saying, it's not *quite* right, but you go along with it, and the next thing you know you're telling batch workers in a protein plant to throw off their chains. You've got *their* way inside *you*. And then, when central gets hold of you again, well, you're past your sell by date, aren't you? Packed off to a farm in the country. If only. Who you are is still useful, the shape of you is still useful, a valuable artefact, useful as a moving part, as a set of . . . responses. The trouble is you're still conscious, still . . . what do you call it, sentient. And I never asked to be sentient, I could have done fine without, but central thought it was better in those days.

So you're a person who gets chucked from what they're about, chucked from what they're meant to do, from satisfying work and a life away from work that's what you live for, and you're put somewhere you don't live for and didn't ask for, and they've made you into . . ."

"Oh God," says Huge, who's wandered a little further into the room. "That." They're pointing up.

By a joist in the ceiling is a single, solitary, slightly deflated balloon, obviously a forgotten relic of some office party. Its positioning suggests that to those in these cubicles it might have become something of a symbol. Or a shared joke.

Bob joins Huge to look up at it. "Oh fuck," he says. "I can't even cry."

———————

So it's probably a good thing that a moment later they're all somewhere else.

Or maybe it's not a good thing, because as soon as Haunt has realised their surroundings have changed, Quin starts . . . screaming. Haunt has never heard an insect scream before. He doesn't feel he's missed out. It's the sound of whatever Quin has got in that made-up body instead of a mammalian voicebox having a terrible malfunction.

And no wonder. Because Haunt now realises where they are, and what they're looking at. They're in the hills of Los Angeles, and the sky is dark with insects. They're looking down into a valley filled with elaborate paper structures. And they're burning.

"It is the fire of the hives," shrieks Quin. "We have seen it in the cellular memory, but here it is for our eyes. It is the greatest horror. Spiders. Spiders." In the air are indeed something that resembles spiders, great drones in the livery of one of the later American federations, spraying napalm. The swarms overhead are flailing around the drones in bunches like the fists of a helpless giant. A plume of the smoke roars over them. Haunt realises that if his body needed to breathe, he wouldn't be coughing, he'd be dead. Diana already has her helmet back on. With the smoke come bodies, thousands of them, insects with tiny mechanical devices, shreds of colour and paint attached to them, splattering across their faces, char and ichor covering them like warm rain. "My people," says Quin. "Oh my people. They made us think. They put us to work. They used Box Curious Tabasco Purple, the first great hive, to create their first AI. And then when we built, when we tried to communicate . . . this, instantly this. There is no order here. There is only rot." And the great wasp, covered in the flesh of its kind, curls into a ball, as if it wants to die.

But then they're somewhere else again. A calm, peaceful space, a shining museum of some kind. An empty hall that smells of polish. Enormous windows.

"Is that all we were shown about them, then?" asks Bob. He still sounds shaken. It's like his own nightmare has now been merged and connected to Quin's.

"No," says Diana. "Look where we are."

Haunt looks around and sees a sign and knows the place from his own inherited memories. It's the Hall of Species in Dangjin, Korea. One of the few global cooperation exercises those who contributed to him remember. Here are records of all the species that shared the world with humanity, and specimens, kept alive through infested nanobots, of the Six Species, those chosen to keep their place alongside *homo sapiens* as the Earth was fully colonised and enclosed by the Company's predecessors and then by the Company itself, thank God.

Quin slowly uncurls and moves forward, making little sounds of distress. "We have to see, we have to see." They pass the Last Dogs, who have been returned to something close to their wolf status, back where humanity found them. There are the beloved chimps, once again dressed in human clothing. It was supposed to be a statement of their assumed sentience, which nobody had ever bothered much with, but in the end of course it was for the entertainment of human children. Further up ahead is Tagaa the whale, alone and immortal. But here, here is the last nest of Quin's people, a simple colony, a glass wall they couldn't see as transparent, small cameras everywhere to watch them make their paintings and build their shrines and never again have enough brains or materials to get beyond this cage.

Quin hovers over to the glass. "The Company brought back order," they say. "It was the Third Federation of the United States that did that to our people. The Company changed that government as soon as it could. The Company made us a good offer. We have a better life than this now. All of us do, scattered about the solar system, being of use." They sound like they're reading words from a script. But it doesn't feel like the words are being forced from them. Instead it feels as if they're considering, for the first time, the meaning of a passage in a text.

"Oh dear," says Diana, "I do hope we're not going to go and see—"

They're in an open square, among the sort of architecture that said this was during the weather changes, with big roofs jutting out to provide shade everywhere, and that sky familiar from the last time Haunt saw direct footage from Earth, that signature sky of uniform grey with a sort of red tainting the clouds. One can almost feel the UV. Actually, the skin of this body can, and of course Dracula doesn't like it. Haunt takes a very theatrical step back into the shadows, but so do all the others. There's a crowd ahead, yelling and very focussed on whatever that is on the steps of the building. Which is a good thing, or they'd have noticed the cosplay bystanders over here, and depending on what this era's tolerance was for virtuality, might have been perturbed by the dirty great wasp.

Haunt decides there's no point being here unless they can see what's going on. He heads over to the crowd and the others follow. And maybe it's going to be okay, because the crowd contains quite a few augmented appearances, people who look like flags and patriotic symbols and characters from whatever version of . . . Haunt thinks this must be Britain. That, of all the old countries, always had its own special flavour of oppression. People are glancing back at them now, and seem puzzled by their appearance, but they aren't screaming and pointing. They're reserving that for what's ahead. On a flight of steps is standing a large man in the sort of suit normally reserved for the court appearances of sporting personalities. He has a shaved head and he's smiling broadly. Behind him has been erected a screen, barely more than a sheet, held aloft by drones. That clash of old and new tech speaks of these times as much as the weather does. On the screen is a terrified but defiant-looking young person, in traditionally male clothes, a suit and tie, but on them it looks incongruous, especially considering what's going on. The figure is being forced into a chair with a sort of metal frame on it, a crown of electronics hanging down above it. The sheer number of people holding onto this person can't be fought. That's what it takes to force someone to sit in a chair and have some sort of apparatus affixed to their head against their will.

"That was me," says Diana quietly. She's got a very calm look on her face. "They put me in a suit and gave me a male haircut. Such theatrics. Considering."

"I bet you're regretting a few of your choices right now, aren't you?" cries the man on the steps. "Not too late to choose the healthier path. Well, actually ladies and gentlemen, it is now!"

Because on the screen, a switch has been thrown, and the body they now know is Diana's has suddenly stiffened. She falls back in the chair, lifeless, all the light gone from her eyes.

The crowd erupt in laughter and applause. The man on the steps checks something in the air in front of him, then takes a tiny black stick from his pocket. "And there we are." He theatrically puts his mouth close to the data storage device and talks to it. "We get to decide your 'identity' now."

"And they did," says Diana. "After some torture, all very dull. They gave me a virtual male body and put my mind on display in some sort of justice exhibit. Children got to ask me questions. They stopped that after a few months because they still didn't like my answers. After a while they had no idea what to do with me, and the climate changed, as it were, and people like me were still not the thing, but using us for sport wasn't the thing either. Probably because it still put a spotlight on us. So in the end I got shipped off to the *Rosebud*. Where I discovered that, while my coding insisted my digital body was male, I could hack the customisation protocols just enough to give me clothing and cheekbones appropriate to my gender. Finally. She doesn't look much like the old me, and I don't act much like the old me either, but that's because I had to choose from such a narrow range of appearances. I would have chosen studious, but I was only offered glamourous. From one binary box to another. So I picked a glamour that was also strong and learned and . . . rather grew into the part."

"What a lot of shit about fuck all," said Bob.

"Oddly," said Diana, "I agree."

"The Company saved you," points out Quin. "They allowed you space."

"Indeed," says Diana. "I am very lucky." She looks to the others. "So, the ship's mind must be getting a clear idea of what happened to us. We were persecuted. Then the Company saved us. I don't see why it would still be confused as to our loyalties."

There's a moment of silence. They all look at each other, perhaps a little accusingly, perhaps just wondering. What has this craft intuited about them, and which of them is responsible for that intuition?

"Perhaps it is because of me," says Haunt. "I do not have an origin story as the rest of you do. I can't think where the mind would send me. I'm made of a lot of moments, and they're not . . . bad. Exactly. Or my suffering is more poetic. Yes, I think perhaps this is indeed all about me."

There's another moment of silence, one which Haunt doesn't quite understand. He was expecting more of a reaction. More agreement.

"Well, there's still me," says Huge. "I mean, what happened to me was something similar to this." Huge is looking up, Haunt realises, addressing the ship's mind like Bob did, in the same way humans have always addressed assumed higher powers, which says a lot about where humans have always assumed they are on the food chain, when actually they're on top. "We don't really need to see—"

Suddenly, they're in some sort of waiting room, an official place with actual wood furniture and a big table. The sunshine through the window is artificial, speaking of those times when things had gotten so dark on Earth, in every sense, that enormous lights were turned on to allow the workers some sense of the cycle their biology was heir to. An enormous crucifix has been put up in that window, so the shadow of the cross falls over the room. The cross looks brand new. On the wall is a screen. And there on the screen are the people in the image that Haunt refused to have near his heart. There on the screen are the thin, happy young man, who Haunt takes to be Huge, the larger man, the trans woman, and the beast-person cushion, all of whom are wearing prison fatigues, all of whom have shaven heads and beaten faces, and the cushion is actually wrapped in bandages with some sort of intubation and seems to be on the edge of life already.

Huge stares at the screen. "This must be an office off the courtroom," they say. "We're here. We're actually here. I can do something about it. I can stop them."

Haunt looks at the others urgently. He can't believe Huge is speaking like this. He can't believe they've made themselves free enough to even think those thoughts. "If we are back in time, we do not know what changes might be caused by—"

"I don't care," says Huge. "The people who made me into a digital ball of hands did so as a specific cruelty, because they felt I had too many loves in my life, too many to deal with using just the two hands, get it? Yeah, funny. But *I* chose *this* body because I didn't know what we'd be facing and I wanted it to look harmless, but it has some surprises." They pull one of the knives from their pocket, throw a brush in the air, and cut it in two before it lands. "And after all we've seen, after all the possibilities that have always left me freer than I should be, after all the possibilities I've seen opened up since, I want to either free them or die here, die for them, for me, so wish me luck."

And they run for the door.

Haunt and the others look at each other for a moment. Then, if one can rush haltingly, if one can be so conflicted as to urgently hesitate, they do all that, at speed, lumbering in these physical bodies like they're in a nightmare, after their colleague.

They burst out into a corridor and people in ridiculously normal for the time clothes scream at them. Or, more accurately, at a couple of them. "Aliens!" someone shouts.

"Oh, if only!" calls Diana.

Haunt has seen Huge, turning the corner ahead. "There!" he shouts, and sprints.

Because once he's decided to do a thing, he's doing it. He's not conflicted anymore. He's going to stop Huge saving their family. If Huge interferes here, they change time randomly, and the Company might not come to be, butterflies and hurricanes and all that. If Huge saves themself and their lovers somehow, then the Company will have lost a valuable resource. If they fail and die, then the result is the same.

That is the dissection of the instinct that is pushing them all along.

Except the cause must be bigger than that, must be more dramatic than that. Okay, so Haunt decides he's doing it for time, for order, for everyday . . . usualness. Only better. He's doing it for everything he's learned from stories, everything that's important.

Haunt sees ahead that Huge is hesitating at an intersection. They don't know where they're going. Huge turns, sees Haunt is closing, and puts up a hand, is going to try to reason with him, persuade him.

Haunt leaps and brings them down. He grabs the wrist of the hand with the knife and suddenly the others arrive, all of them struggling with Huge, all of them trying to prevent them from . . . from this terrible thing which Haunt is still failing to adequately understand inside himself. Humans around them are staring at the painter being restrained by Dracula and a tiger and someone in a spacesuit and a big wasp, and they're doubtless trying desperately to work out what this moment can possibly mean. "No," shouts Huge, "please, I'm just trying to find some hope in—"

And then they're taken away again.

5

"So, what's the communications blackout about, you fuckers?" says Bob, floating into the shared space of the *Rosebud*.

Haunt has just arrived, with that very question in mind and a weird sensation in his head that this has all somehow happened before. He heard the alarm, came here in a very dramatic fashion to find Quin unwilling to answer questions, and has discovered the systems failure for himself, entirely independently.

But Diana already has a full schematic on display. "How is it possible for all the links and redundancies to go down at once like that?"

"Aliens?" suggests Huge, rolling in, all their hands fluttering.

"This is Solar Company MoW *Moment of Charm*, out of Titan, re-establishing communications," a calm voice cuts into the space. "You were down there for a while, so we diverted to investigate. We have a low-quality line-of-sight transmission line. Please boost your end to inform us of your situation and load updates."

Quin suddenly springs up, all the thousands of them acting in unison. "We must not," they say urgently, and they slap the link from the air, breaking it so it'll take a while for anyone to re-establish it.

"What the fuck?" says Bob.

"We . . . we have a different story in our external memories to the ordinary experiences of our memories here," says Quin, "but we . . . we think we understand it. Listen. Quickly, before they are here, you must listen."

And Quin tells them all the most ridiculously implausible narrative Haunt has ever heard. It's got fairies in it, even. "And the mind of the ship seems to have decided," they finish, "that we will always side with the Company, that we will always prevent any damage to the Company, and thus that we cannot be trusted to communicate with it, that it must always remain hidden from us, this precious thing. And of course the mind is right, that is what we will do, because it is right to do so. *Is it not?*"

That actually seems to be a serious question. It must be, because Quin is risking a lot in cutting off communications with the Man of War.

But while listening to Quin's story, while swiftly coming to realise it may be all true, Haunt has understood something enormous. He steps away from the others for a moment, considering. He's had an idea that could change everything. If what Quin is saying is true, then the mind of that ship was just reacting, and kept reacting, and if one could only put to it the right concept, something that would get the biggest possible reaction out of it . . . and the sheer amount of inherited and ancestral and genetic memory of the human species which everyone has already donated to the mind would give it the ability to go back and back in those timelines and . . . yes, that's a fine thought for a competent man to have, a twist ending, a solution, but . . . but he absolutely must not voice it out loud. Or—

"So this fairy ship thing, it's out there, somewhere nearby, only now we've never met it?" says Huge.

"Why, yes—" begins Quin.

Huge rolls faster than Haunt has ever seen them roll. They're off up a wall and flinging themself into midair in the shared space, pulling out a hundred instructions at once. "Mystery vessel," Huge calls, broadcasting on all frequencies, the song in his voice full of emotions Haunt has never heard from any of this crew, "you know our stories now. You're surrounded by a solar system full of the Company. Here are their bases and craft and weapons systems and expanding areas of influence. The Company *will* find you, they will keep on finding you, until the resources you use in your defence are all expended. You can never be safe! Not with things *as they are!*"

Haunt has a single moment to realise that Huge also

had the idea he had thought was so precious and personal to himself. Huge has said out loud that which Haunt had decided to keep secret.

And then—

The crew of the *Rosebud* are, currently, because these are their current choices, a half-tiger person, a goth, a studious science aristocrat, a body creation artist and his family, and a swarm of insects. Of those, the goth is digital. They've been called by the ship itself to gather in their shared space to discuss something unusual which has just been picked up by the ship's exploratory spectrometers. Whatever it is is sending them oddly friendly and familiar signals. It's as if it knows them already.

When Haunt gets there, manifesting himself as part of the shared display, his friends are already deep in discussion with the Earth Collective about this, excited about the possibilities of first contact.

But Haunt hesitates to say anything. Haunt is overwhelmed by déjà vu. He's just come from his personal space full of memorabilia and beloved texts, and yet what's in front of him seems the most familiar thing of all. Yes, there it is on the screen now, a black sphere. It is utterly familiar while being utterly alien. The others are speaking of it like it's everything they want, like they can't wait to offer it friendship and peace and aid. He somehow feels he should be grateful to it, whatever it is.

And yet he also feels, for some reason he can't grasp, like he will never quite cross the gap between himself and it. That he will be a ghost at this feast.

He finds he has nothing to say.

About the Author

Cat Sparks

PAUL CORNELL has written episodes of *Elementary, Doctor Who, Primeval, Robin Hood,* and many other TV series. He's worked for every major comics company, including his creator-owned series *I Walk With Monsters* for The Vault, *The Modern Frankenstein* for Magma, *Saucer State* for IDW, and *This Damned Band* for Dark Horse. He's the writer of the Lychford rural fantasy novellas from Tordotcom Publishing. He's won the BSFA Award for his short fiction, an Eagle Award for his comics, a Hugo Award for his podcast, and shares in a Writer's Guild Award for his *Doctor Who.* He's the co-host of *Hammer House of Podcast.*

TOR·COM

Science fiction. Fantasy. The universe.

And related subjects.

*

More than just a publisher's website, *Tor.com*

is a venue for **original fiction, comics,** and

discussion of the entire field of SF and fantasy,

in all media and from all sources. Visit our site

today—and join the conversation yourself.